LOOK AND FIND®

Disney PRESENTS A PIXAR FILM

Illustrated by Art Mawhinney and Disney Storybook Artists
Written by Caleb Burroughs

Disney/Pixar elements © Disney/Pixar; Dodge is a trademark notice of DaimlerChrysler;
Hudson Hornet is a trademark of DaimlerChrysler; Volkswagen trademarks,
design patents and copyrights are used with the approval of the owner, Volkswagen AG;
Model T is a registered trademark of Ford Motor Company;
Fiat is a trademark of Fiat S.p.A.; Mack is a registered trademark of Mack Trucks, Inc.;
Chevrolet Impala is a trademark of General Motors; Porsche is a trademark of Porsche;
Jeep is a registered trademark of DaimlerChrysler;
Mercury is a registered trademark of Ford Motor Company;
Plymouth Superbird is a trademark of DaimlerChrysler;
Inspired by the Cadillac Ranch by Ant Farm (Lord, Michels and Marquez) © 1974.

Published by
Louis Weber, C.E.O.
Publications International, Ltd.
7373 North Cicero Avenue
Lincolnwood, Illinois 60712

Ground Floor, 59 Gloucester Place
London W1U 8JJ

www.pilbooks.com

Look and Find is a registered trademark of Publications International, Ltd.
p i kids is a registered trademark of Publications International, Ltd.

Manufactured in China.

8 7 6 5 4 3 2 1

ISBN-13: 978-1-4127-3775-3
ISBN-10: 1-4127-3775-3

 publications international, ltd.

Welcome to Radiator Springs! We might be off the beaten path, but there's a whole lot going on in our small town. Cruise around and see if you can spot these cars who live here.

Doc Hudson

Lizzie

Guido

Ramone

Flo

Mater

Welcome to Flo's V8 Cafe. There are always plenty of treats to keep your engine a-purring and your tires a-turning. See if you can find these motor-watering morsels.

Ice Cold Coolant

Mouthwatering Motor Oil

Transmission fluid

Wiper fluid

Anti-Freeze Frosty

Car wax

Lightning McQueen might think he's the only race car in town, but Doc Hudson, the town doctor and judge, has a secret past. He was once a Piston Cup champ! Try to find these memories of Doc's racing days that are hidden in his garage.

Blue ribbon

Plaque

Newspaper article

Flag

Antenna ball

Book

Lightning McQueen might think he's the only race car in town, but Doc Hudson, the town doctor and judge, has a secret past. He was once a Piston Cup champ! Try to find these memories of Doc's racing days that are hidden in his garage.

Blue ribbon

Plaque

Newspaper article

CRASH!
HUDSON HORNET
OUT FOR SEASON

Flag

Antenna ball

CHAMPIONS

Book

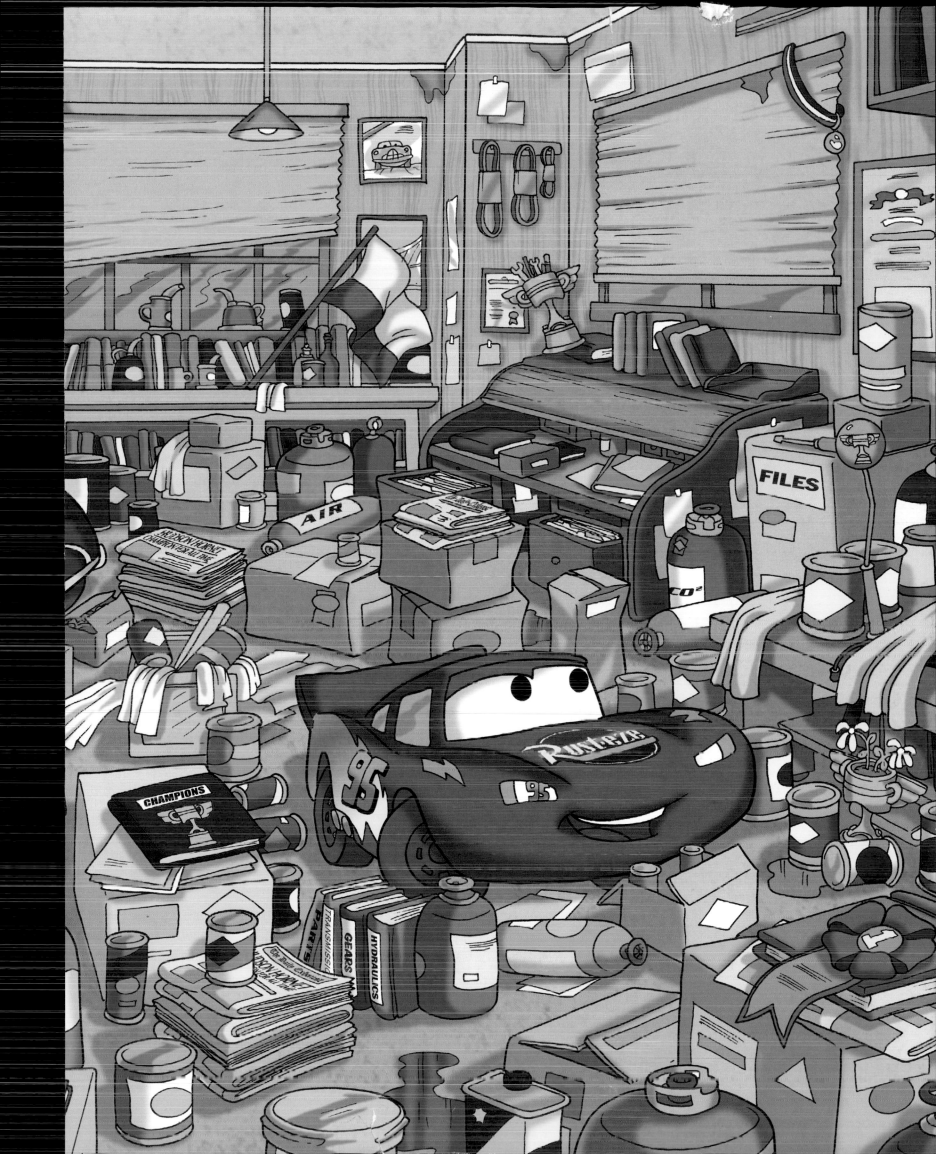

Howdy! My name's Mater and this is my junkyard. Seems I've lost some shiny new pieces in the middle of all these rusty parts. Can you help me find them?

Muffler

Wheel

Tire

Spring

Bumper

Axle

Welcome to Lizzie's Curios Shop. Here you can buy sentimental souvenirs that will remind you of Radiator Springs for years to come. Try to find these fancy license plates.

8675309

A STUDENT

NO.1 DAD

HI MOM

I ♥ U

GO GO GO

Fantastico! Here we are at Luigi's tire shop, where the cars of Radiator Springs get fitted for new tires. See if you can spot some of Luigi's favorite brands.

Fettuccini Crema

Fettuccini Blanco Maximo

Fettuccini Latte

Gripwell Tires

Tread Star

Welcome to the Radiator Springs Courthouse. There is a lot of history here, and most of it has to do with the town's founder, Stanley. See if you can find him in these portraits.

Thank you for stopping by Radiator Springs. Can you find postcards that will help you remember your visit?

Flo's cafe

Doc Hudson's clinic

Mater's junkyard

Lizzie's curios shop

Luigi's shop

Courthouse

Head back to the busy streets of Radiator Springs to find these things you've seen throughout the book.

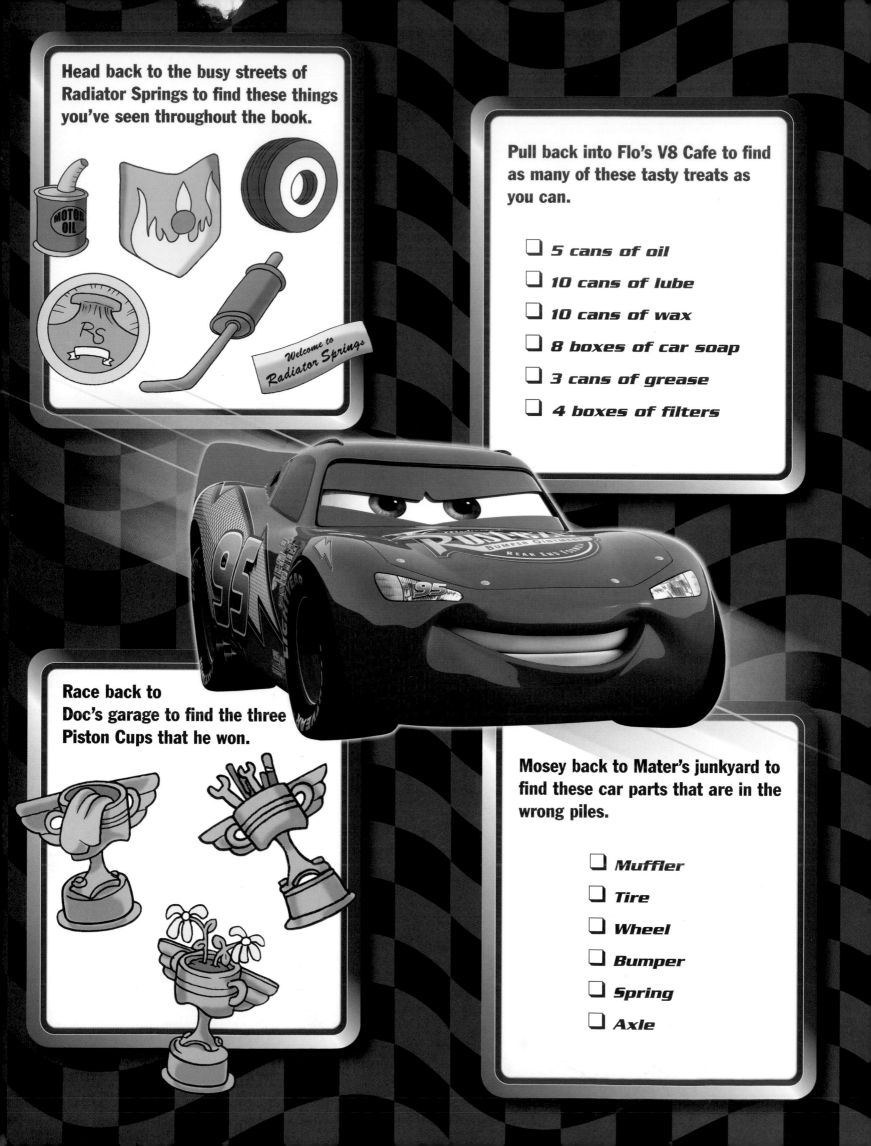

Pull back into Flo's V8 Cafe to find as many of these tasty treats as you can.

- ☐ 5 cans of oil
- ☐ 10 cans of lube
- ☐ 10 cans of wax
- ☐ 8 boxes of car soap
- ☐ 3 cans of grease
- ☐ 4 boxes of filters

Race back to Doc's garage to find the three Piston Cups that he won.

Mosey back to Mater's junkyard to find these car parts that are in the wrong piles.

- ☐ Muffler
- ☐ Tire
- ☐ Wheel
- ☐ Bumper
- ☐ Spring
- ☐ Axle

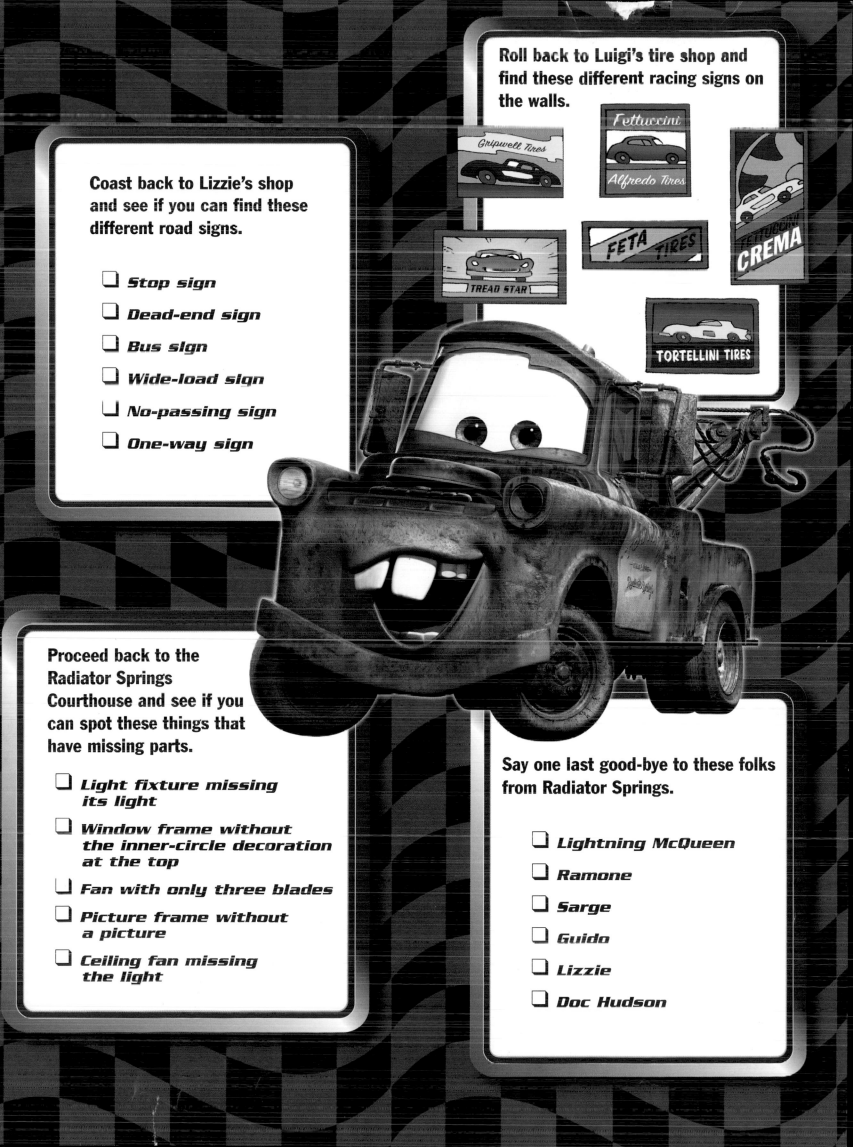

Coast back to Lizzie's shop and see if you can find these different road signs.

- ❏ *Stop sign*
- ❏ *Dead-end sign*
- ❏ *Bus sign*
- ❏ *Wide-load sign*
- ❏ *No-passing sign*
- ❏ *One-way sign*

Roll back to Luigi's tire shop and find these different racing signs on the walls.

Gripwell Tires

Fettuccini Alfredo Tires

FETA TIRES

FETTUCCINI CREMA

TREAD STAR

TORTELLINI TIRES

Proceed back to the Radiator Springs Courthouse and see if you can spot these things that have missing parts.

- ❏ *Light fixture missing its light*
- ❏ *Window frame without the inner-circle decoration at the top*
- ❏ *Fan with only three blades*
- ❏ *Picture frame without a picture*
- ❏ *Ceiling fan missing the light*

Say one last good-bye to these folks from Radiator Springs.

- ❏ *Lightning McQueen*
- ❏ *Ramone*
- ❏ *Sarge*
- ❏ *Guido*
- ❏ *Lizzie*
- ❏ *Doc Hudson*

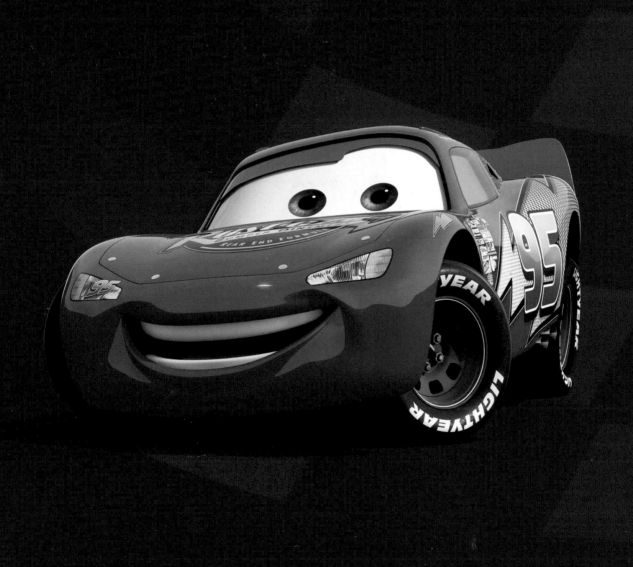